~~CARMICHAEL~~

SDA

NORTHERN IRELAND

by
Gail B. Stewart

CRESTWOOD HOUSE
New York

Collier Macmillan Canada
Toronto

Maxwell Macmillan International Publishing Group
New York   Oxford   Singapore   Sydney

Library of Congress Cataloging-in-Publication Data
Stewart, Gail, 1949-
　　Northern Ireland/Gail B. Stewart. — 1st ed.
　　　　p.　cm. — (Places in the news)
　　Summary: Traces the history of Northern Ireland, focusing on the violence between Protestants and Catholics.
　　ISBN 0-89686-551-7
　　1. Northern Ireland—Juvenile literature. [1. Northern Ireland—History.] I.Title. II. Series: Stewart, Gail, 1949- Places in the news.
DA990.U46S79　1990
941.6—dc20　　　　　　　　　　　　　　　　　　　　　　　　　　　　　　　　90-36291
　　CIP
　　AC

Photo Credits
Cover: Magnum Photos, Inc.: Peter Marlow
Magnum Photos, Inc.: (James Nachtwey) 4, 29, 36; (Stuart Franklin) 13, 26; (Peter Marlow) 32; (Gilles Peress) 43
Culver Pictures, Inc.: 10
AP—Wide World Photos: 16
Marka: (S. Ferraris) 20, 23, 39

Copyright © 1990 Crestwood House, Macmillan Publishing Company

All rights reserved. No part of this book may be reproduced or transmitted in any form or by any means, electronic or mechanical, including photocopying, recording, or by any information storage and retrieval system, without permission in writing from the Publisher.

Macmillan Publishing Company
866 Third Avenue
New York, NY 10022

Collier Macmillan Canada, Inc.
1200 Eglinton Avenue East
Suite 200
Don Mills, Ontario M3C 3N1

Produced by Flying Fish Studio Incorporated

Printed in the United States of America

First Edition

10 9 8 7 6 5 4 3 2 1

CONTENTS

Northern Ireland in the News..5

The Root of the Troubles..8

The Troubles Intensify... 19

Terrorism in Northern Ireland..25

Life in a Troubled Place..35

Facts about Northern Ireland..44

Glossary..45

Index...46

NORTHERN IRELAND IN THE NEWS

Terry McDaid was 29 and had a friendly smile and a thick mop of curly black hair. He and his wife and children lived with his parents in Belfast, the capital of Northern Ireland. Their house was small, in a poor Catholic neighborhood called Tiger's Bay. Terry was unemployed, but he hoped to get a job as a bricklayer soon.

One evening in the spring of 1988, Terry and his wife were relaxing in the living room, enjoying a cup of tea before going to bed. Suddenly two men burst through the door. The men drew guns and shot Terry twice in the head. His wife screamed and tried to strike the men with a piece of a vacuum cleaner lying nearby. The men fled, unharmed, in a stolen car. The car was abandoned soon afterward.

The police of Belfast were confident that the murderers were Protestants and members of a violent military group. However, the motive behind Terry McDaid's murder puzzled the police. Terry had not been a violent man. He had not taken part in any riots or demonstrations in Belfast. In fact, Terry seemed to have had no enemies at all. His friends and family had known him as a devoted father who loved to take his children swimming. Most of his afternoons had been spent out in back of the house, tinkering with the engine of an old car. His murder was, according to the police, a random killing—one in which the killers did not know their victim.

Violent outbursts by angry Catholic and Protestant groups are frequent occurrences in Northern Ireland.

The following evening, in another part of Belfast, a group of Catholic youths—some as young as eight or nine—threw rocks and bricks at the windows of a Belfast police station. One boy of eleven carried a crude bomb he had made from a towel, a glass bottle, and some gasoline. He threw that inside the police station, too. One police officer inside was killed in the explosion; six others were injured.

Such violence by groups of Protestants and Catholics is frighteningly common in Northern Ireland.

"The Troubles"

Northern Ireland is a very small country, approximately the same size as the state of Connecticut. It lies in the northeast corner of an island just west of Great Britain. The rest of the island is called the Republic of Ireland.

But while the Republic of Ireland is a free, independent country, Northern Ireland is not. Northern Ireland, England, Scotland, and Wales make up the United Kingdom of Great Britain. The government of Northern Ireland is controlled by Great Britain, often called, simply, England.

This island of the two Irelands has been known throughout history as the "Emerald Isle" because of its lush, green hills and meadows. When many people think of Ireland, they think of this lovely countryside. They may envision shamrocks or the magical Irish elves called leprechauns. However, the northern part of the Emerald Isle is not filled with beauty and magic. Instead, there are random murders, car bombings, and riots. There are people who hate one another because of their religion or their politics. There

are some people who want to see the country break its ties with Great Britain and unite instead with the Republic of Ireland. There are other people who feel strongly that Northern Ireland should remain part of the United Kingdom. The feelings are so strong, and the hatred runs so deep, that violence has become a way of life in this small country.

The Irish call it "the Troubles." The Troubles, they say, grew worse about 20 years ago. That was in 1969, when British troops were called in to control the fighting between Catholics and Protestants in Northern Ireland. The presence of the British soldiers seems to have made the violence worse, however. Since the arrival of the British soldiers, more than 2,700 people have been killed in Northern Ireland. More than 35,000 have been injured.

Ireland has always been the site of "troubles." But they have become more intense in the past 20 years. The roots of the hatred and the killing go far back. The real source of the problems in Northern Ireland actually can be traced back more than 800 years. The legends, stories, and bad feelings surrounding these long-ago events have been handed down from parents to children, through the generations.

THE ROOT OF THE TROUBLES

Bad feelings between the Irish people and England actually began late in the 12th century. The English themselves had been recently conquered—by a people from northern Europe, called the Normans. Interested in further expanding their kingdom, the Normans looked west, to the island of Ireland.

The Beginning of English Rule in Ireland

In 1171 the Norman king of England, Henry II, came to Ireland with an army of four thousand men. He declared himself the king of all Ireland. The English had fast horses and body armor. They also had powerful catapults and battering rams. The Irish, who were foot soldiers armed only with swords, were no match for King Henry and his troops. They were soon conquered.

Henry II rewarded his leading soldiers, or barons, by giving them huge areas of land. By the 1300s, the Normans held nearly all of Ireland. But, as time went by, the Normans' loyalty to England gradually weakened. By the early 1400s, England actually controlled only a small area around the city of Dublin, called the Pale.

A hundred years later, in 1534, King Henry VIII of England tried to reassert his country's influence in Ireland. He took all power away from some of the strongest Norman lords and tried to control Ireland directly from England. But he met with a lot of resistance. The Irish were organized into fiercely independent tribes, or clans. Each clan had its own king and nobles. They were hard to subdue. Some clans were conquered, but many were able to simply stay out of King Henry's way.

Henry's son, Edward VI, and daughters, Mary I and Elizabeth I, continued to try to subdue Ireland throughout the 16th century.

They are primarily responsible for bringing about the historic animosity between the Irish and the English. In the 1550s, Queen Mary, knowing that the more English people she could settle in Ireland the stronger control she would have, began a policy called the "plantation of Ireland."

She "planted" English men and women on some of the best farmland in Ireland. Many times, the land was already owned by an Irish farmer, but that made no difference to Queen Mary. She ordered her troops to throw the Irish off their land. Sometimes the new English owners would allow the Irish farmers to remain on the land to do some of the difficult, heavy jobs. As the years went by, more and more Irish people were forced off their land by the English. The Irish became angry and resentful.

Protestants versus Catholics

Religious differences between the two peoples were the source of great problems, too. The Irish people were Catholics and had been since Saint Patrick established the first Christian church in Ireland in A.D. 432. However, the English had become Protestants in the 16th century. They wanted every land they conquered to become Protestant, too.

Queen Elizabeth I, who ruled England for nearly half of the 16th century, from 1558 to 1603, used force to make the Irish change their religion. She made it illegal for Catholics to hold prayer services. She executed a number of Catholic priests and bishops. She allowed more land to be seized and given to English farmers. This time it was land belonging to Irish people who refused to give up the Catholic religion.

King James I, Elizabeth's successor, continued to oppress Catholics in the 17th century. Modern-day Catholics in Northern Ireland think of King James as having been extremely cruel to the Irish. He made it his goal to drive every Catholic out of the northern part of the Irish island.

King James offered 500,000 acres of choice farmland to Protestants from Scotland and England who would settle there. Many hundreds of Protestants came to the north of Ireland, eager for a chance to farm its rich, black soil. The Irish were forced off the good farmland. The only land left to them was rocky, or marshy, or simply unfit for farming.

Some Irish Catholics gave in to the pressure of the English kings and queens and became Protestants. However, most of the Irish refused to give up their religion. And while they remained Catholic, their hatred of the English grew stronger and stronger.

The Cruel Penal Laws

Throughout the 1600s, English rulers continued to take more land from the Irish Catholics. By 1704, Catholics held only about a seventh of the land in Ireland. And they were not allowed to purchase, inherit, or even rent land.

To prevent the Irish Catholics from rising up against them, the English tried to keep them poor and powerless. The Catholics were a majority in Ireland. They made up almost 75 percent of the population. However, the power was in the hands of the Protestant

Present-day Irish Protestants demonstrate their support for British control in Northern Ireland. They are the descendants of the British Protestants "planted" in Ireland in the 16th and 17th centuries.

minority. Even though the Protestants were outnumbered, they had control of the country.

The English kings and queens believed that as long as the Irish were poor, as long as they could not read and write, they would not become powerful enough to overthrow their rule. To keep them poor and illiterate, the English passed penal laws. The word "penal" is part of the word "penalty." The penal laws in Ireland, passed in the 18th century, forced penalty after penalty on the Irish people.

The list of things Catholics in Ireland could not do was quite long. They could not vote. They were not allowed to buy any property, including a house or store. They could not run for office or become teachers or lawyers. They weren't allowed to own guns or even a horse worth more than $10!

The English wanted to prevent Irish Catholics from gathering together in groups. They worried that groups of angry Catholics might result in riots or even a full-scale war against the Protestants on the island. For that reason, the penal laws made it clear that any Catholics gathering in groups of four or more would be shot on sight.

The laws also made Catholic schools illegal. Irish mothers and fathers who wanted their children to grow up learning about the Catholic faith had to make a choice. Some families sent their children to Protestant schools and taught them the Catholic faith at home. Some chose not to send their children to school at all. They feared that if the children went to Protestant schools, they might forget their own religion. Many Catholic families sent their children to secret schools that taught about the Catholic faith. These schools were usually held outdoors, in private, secluded spots, for fear that English soldiers or Protestant citizens would find out about them. Held outdoors and in secret, they were sometimes called hedge schools.

Fighting Back

In the late 1700s and early 1800s, many Irish people tried to fight against the injustices of the English rulers. Heroes such as Theobald Wolfe Tone and Robert Emmet are well known to Irish Catholics. They, and others inspired by them, spoke out against the unfairness of the English government. They urged their fellow Irish to revolt—to seek freedom.

In most cases, such heroes were not successful in their struggles for freedom. Most were jailed and executed as traitors or common criminals. Robert Emmet, for instance, was jailed in 1803 after he and his followers tried to capture the center of the English government in Ireland. Emmet and his small army knew they had almost no chance of success. They told their families and friends they expected to die. They felt, however, that by dying in a struggle to free their country, they would be doing an honorable thing. Perhaps, as one of Emmet's followers told his family, their deaths would "bring hope to more good Irish lads to follow their calling." Before Emmet was executed, he gave a stirring speech about freedom, words that were later memorized by thousands of Irish Catholic children. Emmet and other Irish Catholics who were fighting for freedom became martyrs, heroes who willingly died for what they believed.

British guards march along the Dublin Quay with Irish prisoners arrested for participating in the 1916 Easter Rebellion.

Home Rule

As more and more Irish Catholics demanded independence, the English government was forced to listen. In the late 1700s, Catholics were again permitted to own land and to practice their faith. The government refused, however, to grant them any political rights.

By the end of the 19th century, many Irish began to demand "home rule." Under home rule, Ireland would remain part of Great Britain but would control its own domestic affairs.

An Irish journalist named Arthur Griffith formed a political group in 1905 to push for home rule. He named it Sinn Féin. In Gaelic, the language the Irish people spoke before the Normans came, it means "ourselves alone."

Another political group arose around this time also. Known as the Irish Republican Brotherhood (IRB), it was a secret organization that wanted Ireland to be a completely independent republic. Members of the IRB became known as "republicans."

Although the British Parliament finally passed a home rule bill in 1914, the outbreak of World War I prevented it from taking effect. The republicans, led by an Irish Catholic named Patrick Pearse, believed the war gave the Irish a chance to be completely free. They led a revolt against the British in 1916.

Historians call this revolt the Easter Rebellion, because it was supposed to have taken place on Easter Sunday. (As it turned out, delays forced the group to wait until the day after Easter.)

Fighting raged for a week before British forces defeated the rebels. Pearse and the other freedom fighters, like Theobald Wolfe Tone and Robert Emmet before them, knew they were sure to die in the struggle. After taking over several government buildings, including a post office, Pearse and his men signed a proclamation. This proclamation declared all of Ireland free and independent. Pearse and his followers were brave, but they were greatly outnumbered. When the fighting was over, 1,351 were dead, and almost twice as many were wounded. Pearse and 14 other republicans were executed and became new martyrs for the Irish cause.

Partition, but Not a Solution

The execution of the rebels—more than the rebellion itself—created great sympathy among the Irish for the republican cause. Many more people now wanted to be completely independent of England. By 1918, the republicans had gained control of Sinn Féin. In 1919 they declared all Ireland an independent republic. Fighting broke out again between the Irish rebels and British troops.

By 1920 England began to see that the Irish would not give up. The English knew that a change had to be made, so they split Ireland into two very unequal parts. The larger part, made up of 26 counties, was almost entirely Catholic. This part became a dominion, or self-governing country, of Great Britain. It was called the Irish Free State.

The second part was very small. It was formed from 6 counties in Ulster, a large province in the northeastern part of the island. Most of the people in this section were Protestants. They were descended from the Scottish and English farmers "planted" there in the 17th century. These people wanted to remain part of the United Kingdom. England decided to keep control of Northern Ireland, or Ulster, as the Irish also call it.

Even when the Irish Free State gained total independence from Britain in 1949 and became the Republic of Ireland, the Troubles were not over. The country was still divided. And there were many Catholics in Northern Ireland who did not want to remain part of England. They wanted one Ireland, not two. These Catholics sided with their fellow Catholics in the Republic of Ireland, and they have fought against the partition of the island until this day.

THE TROUBLES INTENSIFY

Sometimes when people disagree about how their country should be run, they are able to work out their differences by talking about them. They argue back and forth, each side trying to convince the other.

When, however, people allow strong emotions like fear and anger to take over, no one wants to listen to anyone else. This is what happened in Northern Ireland in 1969. Some people became so angry that they refused to discuss the problems. Instead, they began fighting one another, turning the tiny country of Northern Ireland into a battle zone.

Catholics in Belfast protest for equal rights and, ultimately, an end to British rule.

All Sorts of Discrimination

Independence was not the only issue that the Catholics in Northern Ireland had strong feelings about. They also were angry because they were treated unfairly by the Protestant majority. The government was set up in such a way that the Catholics had no voice at all. The power was divided between the English government in London and the government in Belfast, controlled by Protestants.

Voting was an important area of discrimination. Discrimination is the unfair treatment of one group by a more powerful group. Although some Catholics were able to vote if they owned property (which very few did), the elections were one-sided. Employers were able to cast six or more votes in an election. Since almost all the businesses in Ulster were owned by Protestants, that meant that the Protestant candidates would always win.

Because they had so little power, Catholics of Northern Ireland got very few of the good jobs available. While the unemployment rate in 1967 was 12 percent for Protestants, it was closer to 20 percent for Catholics. Decent housing was impossible for Catholic families to afford. One Catholic resident of Belfast said that most Catholics live in places so small that "you can put your hand down the chimney and open the front door!"

Learning from Dr. King

In 1968 Catholics in Northern Ireland tried a new way to solve their problems. Many of them had followed the newspaper and television news about Dr. Martin Luther King, Jr. They knew he had been working to end discrimination against black people in America. The Catholics of Ulster thought they had much in common with the blacks of the United States.

One of Dr. King's methods was to hold peaceful marches, sit-ins, and protests. The Irish tried the same things. In Belfast and Londonderry, Northern Ireland's two largest cities, thousands of Catholics marched through the streets. They carried large signs and sang American freedom songs like "We Shall Overcome."

Violence Erupts

The peaceful protests made some Protestants angry. During a few of the marches, violence erupted. Secret military groups of Protestants often started trouble. Catholic military groups fought back. There was so much hostility, in fact, that the English government sent in troops to keep order.

At first the Catholics were relieved. They thought that the British soldiers would protect them from the Protestants who threatened them during their protests. One Catholic woman from Belfast remembers taking tea and cakes out to the soldiers on their patrols in the autumn of 1969. "They were our friends," she said. "Or so we thought. As it turned out, we were quite misled."

The soldiers quickly turned their attention from Protestant

A British soldier on patrol in Belfast

terrorists to Catholic terrorists. They spent most of their time driving through poor Catholic neighborhoods, searching for members of the Irish Republican Army (IRA), the secret Catholic military group that developed from the Irish Republican Brotherhood. Soon it was a common sight to see military vehicles rumbling down the streets of the Catholic neighborhoods of Belfast and Londonderry. Local Catholics who had nothing to do with the IRA were furious.

"My father and mother have been roused from their beds at three in the morning. The soldiers say that they're looking for weapons," complained Sean MacDerron, a Belfast Catholic. "Those soldiers have got to know they've come to the wrong house, but they drive the folks out of doors at the point of a gun. Not so much as an 'Excuse me, sir,' or 'Sorry, ma'am.'"

Another resident of Belfast agreed. "I've been stopped and searched as many as three times a week by police. They never do that to Protestants."

The presence of the British soldiers increased the violence. The IRA terrorists suddenly had another reason to strike, and the Protestant terrorists became even more active in response. Neighborhoods put up barbed wire and barricades. Mobs of angry Catholics stormed into Protestant areas, and Protestants invaded Catholic neighborhoods. Hundreds of homes were burned and bombed. Churches, hotels, restaurants, banks, and government offices were gutted and destroyed.

In the 20 years since this round of Troubles began, more than 2,700 people have been killed. Tens of thousands have been injured. One and a half billion dollars in damage has been done. And today there is no sign of an end to the battle.

TERRORISM IN NORTHERN IRELAND

Many people in Northern Ireland believe that terrorists on both sides have increased the hatred. They say that without the terrorists' violence, a solution to the Troubles might have been worked out years ago.

No one knows if that is true. However, it is a fact that besides the British troops in Ulster, there are Catholic and Protestant military groups at war. Quite often the victims of the war are innocent citizens, chosen at random, like Terry McDaid. Both Protestant and Catholic military groups perform these terrorist acts. The heavy death toll among men, women, and children is largely due to the terrorism.

The IRA

The Irish Republican Army is not an official army at all. It has nothing to do with the government of Northern Ireland. It is a secret, military organization. Its members are almost all Catholics who say their goal is to drive the British soldiers out of Northern Ireland. After the soldiers have gone, the IRA says it will fight until the two Irelands are united as one country.

The IRA was first organized to be the military arm of Sinn Féin in 1919. As the years went by, its terrorist acts began to make

A demonstration for NORAID, a group that raises money to support the IRA

many Catholics in Northern Ireland uneasy. They wanted to achieve their goals through peaceful means. The guns and bombs of the IRA would not help that cause. During the next 50 years, the IRA underwent a change. It became less of a military group and more of a social action organization.

But when the British soldiers came to Ulster in 1969, many Catholics were outraged. They were eager to fight back at the British and at the Protestants who had invited the soldiers to come in. Calling themselves the Provisional IRA, or "Provos" for short, this faction of the IRA became more powerful and more violent.

Their methods have been much like those used by guerrilla fighters of other warring nations. They operate secretly, in tiny groups. They surprise their targets and strike anywhere at any time.

When the British soldiers were first sent to Ulster in 1969, they were told never to fire if there was the slightest chance of hitting a bystander. The Provos have taken advantage of that. They often hide behind crowds of people and then take shots at the soldiers. They know the British cannot fight back without hitting innocent people in the crowds.

Powerful, but Not Large

The Provisional IRA is greatly feared by the British, for its members have caused the deaths of many hundreds of British soldiers and Irish Protestants. Yet, although it is very powerful, the Provos are not a large group.

The government of Northern Ireland believes that the group has no more than 300 members. There are 50 or 60 at the core of the organization. It is their job to make military plans and choose the next target for violence. Besides the small core group, there are about 200 "active service" members. They are the men and women who do the actual shooting and bombing.

Although the Provos sometimes kill people at random, many of their targets are very well known. In 1979, for instance, the IRA killed British hero Lord Mountbatten, a relative of Queen Elizabeth. In 1984 they set off a bomb in England that nearly killed British Prime Minister Margaret Thatcher.

"More Weapons Than They Know What to Do With"

One official in the Ulster police force has been quoted as saying that no one will ever outshoot the Provos. "They have too many sophisticated weapons—more weapons than they know what to do with," he said. When the Provos first became active, they had no money to buy weapons. They depended on IRA members to smuggle guns from other countries, especially the United States.

In the past 20 years, however, the IRA has become far more organized. It gets high-tech weapons from the Soviet Union and Libya. In October 1987, British government agents seized a ship

The IRA uses many terrorist methods, including random bombings, in its fight to make Northern Ireland free from British control.

that they thought was carrying illegal drugs. Instead, they found more than 150 tons of weapons bound for Northern Ireland from Libya. Officials later learned that before this ship was seized, four others were able to make their deliveries.

The ship was carrying many kinds of weapons. There were surface-to-air missiles, grenade launchers, automatic rifles, and explosives.

How Do They Pay for It All?

The IRA needs between $8 and $12 million per year to pay for its terrorist acts. Much of the money is used to buy weapons. Each member of the Provos is paid a small amount every week—between $35 and $40. Where does all this money come from?

In 1970 the IRA set up the Irish Northern Aid Committee (NORAID) to raise money in the United States. There are about 20 million Irish-Americans, many of them in the northeastern part of the United States. Some Irish-Americans feel strong ties with the land of their heritage. Some have relatives who still live in Ulster. In 1970 NORAID raised more than $3 million in the United States!

It might seem surprising that a terrorist organization would get so much support. However, most Americans aren't aware that the money they give is going to the IRA. NORAID claims that the money goes to help widows and children in Northern Ireland.

Fund-raising by NORAID has supplied only part of the money needed by the Provos, however. Some of the money has come from illegal drug sales and robberies in both Northern Ireland and the Republic of Ireland. Stores and other businesses are forced by IRA soldiers to pay "protection money." This is money owners pay each month to the IRA so that the Provos do not vandalize or burn their businesses.

Recently, however, the IRA has been able to raise money legally. The IRA owns several businesses, including a large fleet of taxis, video stores, and restaurants. These ties to legitimate businesses give the IRA a more secure economic base.

In the Maze

The Provos have learned to create support and sympathy for their cause. Most of the Provos who are arrested for terrorism are put in a Belfast prison called the Maze. At the Maze, hundreds of IRA soldiers are spending ten, twenty, or all of the remaining years of their lives. They pass the time in concrete cells. Even in prison, the Provos have organized their cell blocks into military rankings. In each block, there is a commander, a second-in-charge, and so on.

The prisoners believe that they should be handled in a different manner from the common criminals. They consider themselves "political prisoners." They are in prison, they say, only because their political ideas are different from the government's. As political prisoners they should, for example, be allowed to wear their own clothing instead of prison uniforms.

The officials at the Maze think otherwise. They believe, as does the British government, that the IRA soldiers are common criminals and that they should be given no special treatment.

"Lads of the Blanket" and Hunger Strikers

To protest what they feel is unfair treatment, many IRA prisoners have gone "on the blanket." They refuse to wear any clothes at all, even though the cells are very cold. They wrap themselves only in gray prison blankets. They refuse to bathe. They do not shave, letting their beards and hair grow very long. Some of the prisoners smear food and their own body wastes on their cell walls. In the eyes of many Ulster Catholics, these "lads of the blanket" have become martyrs. People speak with sorrow of their terrible prison conditions.

However, no IRA protest has generated as much emotion and sympathy as the hunger strike. A hunger strike occurs when a prisoner simply refuses to eat. Since a person can survive without food for only a limited time, eventually the prisoner will die.

The first IRA hunger striker was a 27-year-old named Bobby Sands. In 1981 he decided he could attract worldwide attention to the cause of the IRA with a hunger strike. He wanted people to know how intensely the IRA wanted a united, free Ireland.

Bobby Sands lived for 66 days without food. Starvation is very painful. Thousands of people begged Sands to stop his hunger strike. He continued, however, enduring violent stomach cramps, deafness, and blindness before he died.

When Catholics heard the news that Sands had died, many wept openly in the streets. Children prayed for him, and special masses were said at Catholic churches. About 50,000 people attended his funeral!

A young woman displays her support for Bobby Sands, an imprisoned IRA member who died after a 66-day hunger strike.

Since Bobby Sands's death, hundreds of other IRA prisoners have gone on hunger strikes. As one IRA soldier said, "We will continue to do whatever it takes. We cannot afford to lose. We will keep the campaign going, regardless of the cost to ourselves, regardless of the cost to anyone else."

Not the Only Terrorists

The IRA is not the only group of terrorists bombing and killing people in Ulster. There is a secret military group of Protestants, too. It is called the Ulster Defense Association (UDA). The UDA is made up of small groups that are like gangs.

The history of the UDA is much like that of the IRA. It was created to show how intensely the Protestants hate the rebellious Catholics and how determined they are to put them down. Its methods are as cruel and violent as those used by the Provos.

Over the past two decades, UDA members have become infamous for torturing their victims. They have hunted down Catholics and slit their throats. Sometimes the UDA members have bound the hands of their victims and shot them in their heads, gangland-style. Sometimes, just to "teach a lesson," UDA members "kneecap" their targets. Kneecapping is a sharp, painful injury to a person's kneecap, a very delicate bone. Often bullets are used; other times metal rods or even power drills do the damage. The idea is to make the victims remember their fear and pain for the rest of their lives.

Both the Provos and the UDA have attacked victims at random. The Provos have stormed into Protestant areas and gunned down men walking along the street. The UDA has planted bombs in grocery stores in Catholic neighborhoods. Occasionally the IRA and the UDA attack each other. When this happens, neither group wants to claim responsibility. There are cries of "they started it" on both sides.

Whichever side is to blame on a particular day does not seem to matter. The result of the terrorism is a country where violence and death have become almost routine. The day-to-day life of the people of Ulster is a tragic reflection of the Troubles there.

LIFE IN A TROUBLED PLACE

The Protestants of Northern Ireland want very much to remain part of the United Kingdom. The Catholics want just as much to break away. As you learn more about the problem, you may find that both the Protestants and the Catholics have good arguments.

The Catholics argue that Ireland was once all one land, all Catholic people. They recall the English kings and queens who stole their land and drove them away. They argue that they have been discriminated against for centuries in their own land. England, they feel, has no right to keep control of Northern Ireland.

A bomb thrown by an IRA terrorist blows up a British "pig," an armored car designed especially to protect British soldiers in Northern Ireland.

The Protestants admit that what the kings and queens of England did was wrong. However, they argue, that was hundreds of years ago. The Protestants of modern-day Ulster did not do those cruel things. They consider themselves Irish, not English—they have been farmers in Ulster for generations. If Northern Ireland were to be united with the Republic of Ireland, the Protestants would become a weak minority, subject to a powerful Catholic majority. That idea makes them very uncomfortable.

Peace Walls and "Pigs"

There are now 16,000 British troops and 13,000 Ulster police in Northern Ireland. The land looks like a battleground, although Northern Ireland is at war with no one. This is especially true of its capital, Belfast.

Some of Belfast is lovely. It is dotted with parks and green, rolling fields. On nice days, families have picnics and teenagers play soccer. Some visitors to Belfast can forget about the Troubles if they stay in these places. However, the moment they walk near the poor sections of the city (especially the Catholic areas), everything changes.

British troops are everywhere. They walk through the streets with guns drawn, especially when they've heard a rumor about IRA activity. They drive down the streets in olive-colored vehicles called "pigs." A pig carries eight soldiers and is built to be almost bomb-proof. It was designed especially for duty in Northern Ireland.

Catholic neighborhoods are separated from Protestant ones by "peace" walls. These massive, 12-foot-high walls are bullet-chipped and often have graffiti on them. Slogans such as UP THE IRA and THANK GOD I'M A PROD (Protestant) decorate their drab sides. The barriers were built during the Troubles of 1969 by the government, which thought separating the two groups would help keep peace.

Catholic Ghettos

A ghetto is an area where people who have the same culture live together. Usually ghettos are located in the poor sections of town. That is the case in Belfast. The Catholics, who have less money than the Protestants, live in the poorest sections of the city.

The Catholic ghettos are almost empty of cars, since few people there can afford them. Many people live in government-owned housing projects. These are much the same as the housing projects in some American cities.

Since there are so many people and so few houses, many large Catholic families are cramped into homes built for one or two people. Quite often there is no central heating. Roofs leak and pipes back up, and the landlords refuse to fix them. Rats and mice scurry everywhere. In some neighborhoods, almost 40 percent of the people are without jobs. It is easy to see why many of the Catholics in these areas are unhappy.

Furthermore, many of the IRA members live in these areas, so British troops are always nearby. Closed-circuit cameras are aimed at buildings and street corners where young people gather. The government wants to keep an eye out for troublemakers.

A Belfast "peace" wall, built to separate Catholic and Protestant neighborhoods

British soldiers have an extremely difficult job in Northern Ireland. They are supposed to make sure there is no violence. However, their very presence is annoying to Catholics. People in these ghettos call the soldiers names. They swear at the soldiers and taunt them. Often very young children spit at them or hurl rocks.

Stress and Anxiety

The Troubles have taken a toll on many of the children of Ulster. The constant sound of gunfire scares them. The presence of so many soldiers and police worries them. The sight of barbed wire on their school-yard fences frightens them. So, too, does the constant talk they hear from parents and friends about the Troubles.

These things affect the children in many different ways. Some children have become sullen and angry. Their teachers have a hard time controlling them in school. Said one teacher in a Catholic grade school, "How can we hope to make them mind? They are seven and eight in their bodies, but they're as old as the hills. They've seen it all. They know the sound of blood running in the street, of guns and bombs. They're up half the night shouting at soldiers. They have no use for authority, least of all mine!"

Some children are very quiet. They may have trouble speaking without stuttering. Some wet their beds at night or cry all the time. Psychologists, people who study human behavior, say that such reactions are normal. Children who have been under as much stress and nervous strain as the children of Northern Ireland are bound to be anxious.

A few children are lucky enough to leave the terror of Belfast for a few weeks. There are programs in the United States in which young Irish boys and girls can visit American families during the summer. Catholic children are placed with Protestant families. Protestant children stay with Catholic families. The few weeks without gunfire, bombs, or angry mobs of people—and the chance to get to know that there are good people of both faiths—can be very healthy.

Hope?

Another sad effect of the Troubles is the lack of hope many children feel. The Troubles have been going on all their lives. They do not know what a peaceful world is. Because life is so uncertain, many young people have not allowed themselves to dream about a brighter world.

However, there are glimmers of light that the hatred is lessening. One such clue is that many Catholics and Protestants alike are tired of the senseless killing. So many innocent people, including young children, have been killed in the Troubles that people are sickened by it. Many people think that if the terrorists on both sides would stop the violence, reason might prevail.

Another hopeful sign is that some well-known Irish-Americans are speaking out against the violence. For many years, American politicians tried to stay out of the whole argument. Some did not want to offend England, one of America's chief allies. Others did not want to anger millions of Irish-American voters.

Recently, however, Senators Edward Kennedy and Daniel Moynihan, former Speaker of the House Thomas "Tip" O'Neill, and former Governor of New York Hugh Carey have been speaking up. They have urged people not to give money to organizations such as NORAID, which might buy weapons. Instead the U.S. government gives money to Northern Ireland to create jobs there. Over the past three years, more than $120 million have provided 4,500 permanent jobs in the poorest sections of Ulster.

Many people think that economic help is a good beginning to ending the Troubles, especially in Catholic neighborhoods. "People aren't as likely to go about busting windows when they've got windows of their own," commented one Catholic woman. "If you've a nice home and family, and a life worth living, you aren't going to be out looking for trouble."

However, those who live in Ulster are not counting on a quick solution. The hate runs so deep that it shows up in the most innocent places. When small children at a Protestant school in Belfast jump rope, they chant:

If I had a penny, do you know what I'd do?
I would buy a rope and hang the pope.

And less than a half mile away, young Catholic children are jumping rope, too. Their chant is just as full of hate:

Saint Patrick's Day will be jolly and gay,
And we'll kick all the Protestants out of the way.
If that won't do, we'll cut them in two
And send them to hell with their red, white, and blue.

Children are perhaps the greatest victims of the conflict in Northern Ireland.

FACTS ABOUT NORTHERN IRELAND

Capital: Belfast

Population: 1.5 million

Form of government: A constitutional monarchy; part of the United Kingdom

Official language: English

Chief products:
  Agriculture: eggs, hogs, milk, potatoes, cattle
  Manufacturing: Irish linens, alcoholic beverages, aircraft, ships, and canned goods

Glossary

discrimination *The unfair treatment of one group by a more powerful group.*

ghetto *A part of a city where the people of one race or nationality live together. Ghettos are usually poor sections of a city.*

hedge schools *Secret Catholic schools often held outdoors in Ireland when England outlawed Catholic schools.*

hunger strike *A form of protest in which a person refuses to eat unless his or her demands are met.*

martyr *One who dies or otherwise suffers for a particular cause.*

"on the blanket" *A form of protest in which jailed IRA members refuse to wear regular prison clothing. They wrap themselves instead in blankets.*

partition *A division; in 1920 Ireland was partitioned into two countries.*

"peace" walls *Massive walls that separate Catholic and Protestant sections of Belfast.*

penal laws *A group of harsh laws the English imposed on the Irish Catholics in the 18th century; they were designed to keep the people poor and powerless.*

plantation of Ireland *A system begun by Queen Mary I in the 1550s. She evicted Irish farmers from their land and "planted" English and Scottish farmers in their places.*

"the Troubles" *The term for the violence between Catholics and Protestants in Northern Ireland.*

Index

Belfast 5, 6, 20, 21, 22, 23, 24, 31, 37, 38, 39, 41, 42

Carey, Hugh 42
Catholics 5, 6, 8, 11, 12, 14, 15, 17, 18, 19, 21, 22, 24, 25, 27, 33, 34, 35, 37, 38, 39, 40, 41, 42

Easter Rebellion 16, 17
Edward VI 9
Elizabeth I 9, 11, 12
Emmet, Robert 15, 17
England (Great Britain) 6, 8, 9, 11, 12, 17, 18, 19, 37, 41

ghetto 38, 40

hedge schools 15
Henry II 9
Henry VIII 9
home rule 17
hunger strike 33, 34

Irish-Americans 30, 41

Irish Free State 18, 19
Irish Northern Aid Committee (NORAID) 26, 30, 42
Irish Republican Army (IRA) 24, 25, 26, 27, 28, 30, 31, 33, 34, 35, 36, 37, 38
Irish Republican Brotherhood (IRB) 17, 24

James I 12

King, Dr. Martin Luther, Jr. 22
"kneecapping" 34

"lads of the blanket" 33
Libya 28, 30
Londonderry 22, 24

martyr 15, 18, 33
Mary I 9, 11
Maze, the 31
McDaid, Terry 5, 25

Mountbatten, Lord 28
Moynihan, Daniel 42

Normans 9, 17
Northern Ireland 5, 6, 8, 12, 13,
 19, 21, 22, 25, 27, 28, 30, 31,
 35, 36, 37, 40, 42, 43

O'Neill, Thomas "Tip" 42

"peace" walls 37, 38, 39
Pearse, Patrick 17, 18
penal laws 12, 14
"pigs" 36, 37
plantation of Ireland 11
Protestants 5, 6, 8, 11, 12, 13, 14,
 15, 18, 21, 22, 24, 25, 27, 34,
 35, 37, 38, 39, 41, 42
Provos 27, 28, 30, 31, 34

Republic of Ireland 6, 8, 19, 31,
 37

Saint Patrick 11, 42
Sands, Bobby 33, 34

Scotland 6, 12
Sinn Féin 17, 18, 25
Soviet Union 28

Thatcher, Margaret 28
Tiger's Bay 5
Tone, Theobald Wolfe 15, 17
Troubles, the 6, 8, 19, 24, 25,
 35, 37, 38, 40, 41, 42

Ulster 18, 19, 21, 22, 25, 27,
 28, 30, 33, 34, 35, 37, 40,
 42
Ulster Defense Association
 (UDA) 34, 35
United Kingdom 6, 8, 19, 35
United States 22, 28, 30, 41

Wales 6